The Steel Whale

First published in 2012
by Wayland

Text copyright © Tom Easton 2012
Illustration copyright © Woody Fox 2012

Wayland
338 Euston Road
London NW1 3BH

Wayland Australia
Level 17/207 Kent Street
Sydney, NSW 2000

Series Editor: Louise John
Series design: D. R. ink
Design: Lisa Peacock
Consultant: Shirley Bickler

A CIP catalogue record for this book is available from the British Library.

ISBN 9780750268639

Printed in China

Wayland is a division of Hachette Children's Books,
an Hachette UK company
www.hachette.co.uk

The Steel Whale

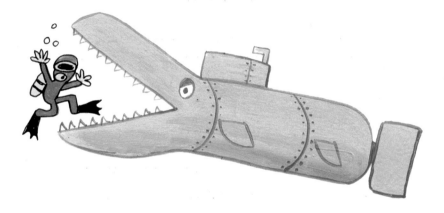

Written by Tom Easton
Illustrated by Woody Fox

WAYLAND

It was a quiet morning on the seabed. Sea Force Four had just eaten breakfast.

Suddenly there was a whoosh of bubbles and the clam phone rang.

Blob Pufferfish got there first.
"Hello?" he said.

"Help!" cried a voice. "Something
has dropped on top of us!"

It was one of the sea urchins.

"Oh, no!" said Blob. "Are you ok?
Is anyone hurt?"

"I don't think so," said the sea
urchin, "but we are trapped!"

Sea Force Four raced to help the sea urchins. Zip Marlin got there first. He was super-speedy.

"It's a whale," Zip told the others as they swam up, panting.

"No," replied Polly Porpoise, tapping it with her tail. "It's made of steel."

"A steel whale?" Zip cried.

"It's hard to see in the dark," Polly said. "Luna...?"

"I know," Luna Lampfish said. "You want me to shine my light."

"Look," said Blob. "It's like a mirror.
I can see myself!"

Zip whizzed over the top and peered into a bent tube.

He saw a pair of eyes looking back at him. "There's something inside here!" he called to the others.

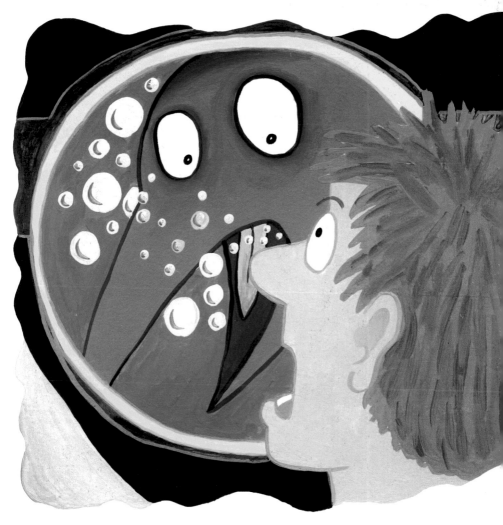

Just then Blob saw a face.
"Humans!" he cried.

He puffed up like a balloon and
zoomed off to hide behind the coral.

"Come on everyone," Polly said.
"They need help."

"But they are humans," Blob said.
"They are the ones who keep
dropping things into the water."

"They don't mean to hurt us," Polly told them. "Now they're trapped and scared, just like the sea urchins."

"But what can we do to help them?" Luna asked.

"Shine your light over here," Polly said. "Look! The whale's tail is trapped in the rocks."

Sea Force Four began to move the rocks. It was hard work.

Blob was very strong. Zip and Polly flipped rocks away with their tails, and Luna shone her light.

At last the steel whale was free.
Sea Force Four backed away as it
rose off the sea bed.

The humans in the windows smiled. They waved and set off into the deep dark water.

"How did the humans get inside the whale?" asked Zip. "Did the whale swallow them?"

"Oh, Zip," said Blob.
"I'll tell you later!"

START READING is a series of highly enjoyable books for beginner readers. **The books have been carefully graded to match the Book Bands widely used in schools.** This enables readers to be sure they choose books that match their own reading ability.

Look out for the Band colour on the book in our Start Reading logo.

Pink Band 1

Red Band 2

Yellow Band 3

Blue Band 4

Green Band 5

Orange Band 6

Turquoise Band 7

Purple Band 8

Gold Band 9

START READING books can be read independently or shared with an adult. They promote the enjoyment of reading through satisfying stories supported by fun illustrations.

Tom Easton is an experienced author of children's books, including lots of funny Start Reading books about the Poor Pirates! He lives with his family in Surrey.

Woody Fox has been illustrating children's books for 18 years! He was born in London, but now lives in a cute thatched cottage in the middle of Devon with his 2 cats. When he's not drawing, he likes to do mosaics, basket weaving and go for long walks!